Dancin' in the Rain

YASMIN WHIRL

PUBLISHED BY
OUR WRITTEN LIVES, LLC

Our Written Lives, LLC provides publishing services for authors in various educational, religious, and human service organizations. For information, visit www.OurWrittenLives.com.

Library of Congress Cataloging-in-Publication Data
Whirl, Yasmin
Dancin' in the Rain
Library of Congress Control Number: 2020920509
ISBN: (paperback) 978-1-942923-44-2

Contents

Dedication

I dedicate this book to every pregnant teenager I have counseled and listened to as a High School Counselor. I dedicate this book to every teenage father as well. Teenage fathers are often overlooked during the pregnancy process, but they also have both hopes and fears, and want what is best for the baby.

I dedicate this book to every teenage parent I don't know personally. I pass you in the stores, I see your pics on social media, and my heart goes out to you. Hang in there. You will get through it. Your life has changed forever but pick up the pieces and let your journey paint your story.

In 2017, a total of 194,377 babies were born to women aged 15–19 years old in the United States. That is a birth rate of 18.8 per 1,000 women in this age group. The statistic is a record low for U.S. teens. Still, the U.S. teen pregnancy rate is substantially higher than any other western industrialized nation (Centers for Disease Control and Prevention, 2017).

Acknowledgments

Who would have known that the year 2020 would bring a global pandemic, the Coronavirus COVID-19? Our world changed quickly before our eyes. Death, sickness, unemployment, canceled events, and working remotely from home has shaken our nation and impacted the world. This year has been something that we could not control, and that we still don't fully understand.

During my time at home, God whispered into my ear and told me it was time to write again. I love to write, but I have to get in a mindset to do so. It is sometimes hard for me to focus on writing because I am so busy, but the Lord slowed me down. I locked myself up in my office and wrote, but God gave the story.

Introduction

Tap. Tap. Tap. Tap.
One. Two. Three. Four. Five. Six. Seven. Eight.
One. Two. Three. Four. Five. Six. Seven. Eight.
Tap. Tap. Tap. Tap.
Let's try it again.
One. Two. Three. Four. Five. Six. Seven. Eight.
Move to the left three times.
Move to the right three times.

Music moves my body. I feel the beat. I feel the vibe, and I move. My arms move. My feet move. My hands move. My head moves. I leap into the air. I move by creation. I move by nature. I move.

Let's go. Let's dance.
Can you feel it? Can you feel it?
Let's dance. Let's swing. Let's ballet.
Let's step. Let's leap.

Stop!

My body and feet want stop, but I keep moving. The routine is simple and easy. I catch on the first try every time. It's not challenging to me at all.

I flow as I dance. I flow with music. I hear the sound. I hear the beat. I hear the move.

Welcome to Ieshia's world. It's a world of dance. A world of freedom. A world of escape. Welcome to Ieshia's world. Do you want to come and hang with me?

The ride can get a little rocky. I am unorthodox. I am the black sheep of my family. I do nothing right. I am a PK. That's right, a "Preacher's Kid."

Do you want more? Can you handle Ieshia's world?

I am 16 when my story begins, and no one can tell it better than me.

Welcome Home

Chapter 1

"Welcome home!"

I never thought I would hear those words from Bishop Michael Harvey, a.k.a. Dad, a.k.a. "The Terminator!"

Did I say that? That's how I felt when he shipped me off ten years ago after my mom told him I was six weeks pregnant, sixteen, and as scared as all get out. My new home was with my Dad's oldest sister, Aunt Velma, in Atlanta, Georgia.

And now he has the audacity to say, "Welcome home!" Really?! Some Bishop Dad you are! Believe it or not, I forgave him a long time ago, but he never gave me the opportunity to explain what happened, and that eats at my soul.

All he said back then was that I had *"defiled the kingdom of God by fornicating"* and that I must *"leave immediately."*

He has aged since then and has a head full of gray hair. He is still preaching and teaching the Gospel. Who he is hasn't changed much.

Now, with excitement in his voice, Dad says, "There is my grandson, Malcolm! Hey bud! I have missed you and can't wait to get to know you!" Dad gives Malcolm a big hug.

As he puts my son down, Malcolm says, "Hey, Granddad. What's up? Want to see me dance?" Malcolm starts dancing, just like I did when I was his age.

Dad chuckles and says, "Maybe later. I have to retire back to my study to prepare for Sunday's sermon." He leaves the living room and heads into his office.

"There goes my grandson!" Mom says with excitement as she comes out from the kitchen wearing her yellow apron.

With a big smile, Malcolm says, "Hey, Grandma! I love you and can't wait to eat your collard greens and cornbread. Mom says you can really cook."

Mom gives Malcolm a really big hug. She always called and checked on me, and often wrote me letters. She knows every detail about her grandson and what he has been up to since his birth in 2010.

He is a smart, energetic, and a typical boy. My parents had two girls, so he was a prayer answered. My life changed dramatically when I had him and I have not looked back since. My life is better with him in it.

I hadn't planned on packing us up and moving back to Dublin, leaving our memories behind in Atlanta. I now have to face what shipped me off—my dad, my truth. Let's rewind this show, back ten years. Back to where I started my life and journey as Bishop Harvey's youngest daughter, Ieshia, 16 and pregnant.

• • •

"Ieshia Sarah Harvey, what are you doing?" Mom sighed. "It's time for church!"

"Mom, we go all the time!" I pouted. "Can I stay home today?"

"No! It's the church anniversary. Get dressed so we can go!"

Mom put her hands on her hips. She was getting frustrated with me. That happened all of the time, really. Reluctantly, I said, "Yes, ma'am."

"Ieshia. Turn that music off and get dressed," Mom said again a few minutes later.

I was dancing to *Fancy* by Drake. It was his debut album and it was hot. My mouth, as always opened wide and sarcastically as I said, "Maybe Bishop Harvey will let me try out for the dance team at school this year. I am 16 now. Its time." I stood firm, tall, and rolled my neck.

Mom gave me that look. I knew what she meant by that look. She hated it when I referred to Dad as "Bishop Harvey" while we are home.

"Okay. Maybe . . ." I started speaking extremely slow, emphasizing the next word. ". . . *Dad* will let me try out for the dance team at school this year. I am 16 now. Its time!"

At the top of her lungs, Mom shouted, "Ieshia! You know his beliefs about dancing outside of worship. Liturgical dance only!"

At the age of 16, I would not let it go. I had a good argument, but I knew my mom would tear my butt up if I continued. Still, I had to have the last word. "Okay! Forget it!"

Mom came upstairs, grabbed my belt from the closet and said, "I am going to get on your butt! For the last time, get dressed and be downstairs in fifteen minutes!" She won, as always. She is the boss.

"Yes, ma'am."

"Ieshia," my sister called me from her bedroom across the hall. She said she just wanted to check on me, but really, she was just being nosy. She heard the entire conversation.

"Yes, Patrice," I responded reluctantly.

"Are you ready?" She asked as she walked into my bedroom.

"Yes, Mrs. Sanders—I mean, Lady Sanders!"

Patrice was 21 and engaged to the church Youth Pastor, Minister David Sanders. Patrice smiled, twirled around in her long, red, maxi dress, and almost fell over.

I chuckled and said, "Leave the dancing to me, Sis! Okay? What song are you singing today?"

Patrice was the singer in the family; she still is.

"I'll be singing, *Having You There* by the Mississippi Mass Choir.

I decided to wear my long red maxi dress too. I quickly finished getting dressed and Patrice and I headed downstairs together.

We loaded into the back of Dad's Black Cadillac to head to Faith Tabernacle Missionary Baptist Church. Before Dad pulled out of the driveway, he said, "Let's pray. Ieshia, lead prayer today."

I sigh. *Of course*, I thought to myself. "Dear God, keep us safe in this old vehicle. Amen."

"Ieshia!" Mom said from the front seat.

Dad shook his head and prayed again, "Heavenly, Father, anoint us with your precious love and keep us safe on the highway as we travel to church and back. In Jesus' name we pray . . ."

And everyone said, "AMEN!"

The church anniversary was a time for us to commemorate the founding of the church and to give accolades to the great accomplishments that have happened since then. 100 years really was a long time for a church to stay open and active. It was a reason to celebrate.

Dad, or should I say Bishop Harvey, had been the pastor for the past 20 years. The church absolutely loved him! Dad was really cool, handsome, and could sing.

But as a Dad, he was really strict. I kinda get it because of his role, but good grief. I was a teenager, and just liked to have fun. We went to church all of the time! I knew the Bible. Dad thought I didn't because I talk all the time, and love to dance, but I really knew and loved God! I still do.

There she went. Patrice was singing Dad's favorite song. He rocked side to side in the pulpit while her fiancé, David Sanders, stood up to worship. There you had it. Patrice always shouted when she sang. She a powerhouse!

Mom stood up to worship, raising her hands as she sang.

Dad loved seeing his family giving their all to worshipping God.

As for me, just let me dance! I would shut the service down with my skills! I started laughing as I watched some of the people around me, and Mom gave me that firm look. I dropped my head and covered my mouth.

It was a long day at Faith Tabernacle Missionary Baptist Church. The deaconesses flocked to their corner with their white feathered hats and long white dresses. They sort of reminded me of a bunch of hens with ruffled feathers.

The deacons proceeded to lead devotions in their black pinstripe suits. I can't forget to mention Dad's armorbearers, who waited on him hand and foot. They served as his assistants at the church and often traveled for weekly revivals both locally and out of town. I knew it's their role, but I always felt like they took it too far.

Well, that was the recap of my day. We went back home, and Mom was in the kitchen preparing Sunday Dinner.

"Ieshia," she said. She stopped cooking and looked at me as I started to head up the stairs.

"Yes, ma'am?"

"Where are you goin'?"

"Up to my room," I said.

"Stop running."

I wanted to argue with her this time, so I stopped in my tracks on the fourth step of the stairs and turned around to face her head on.

"We have been in church all day long. May I please go to my room?" I say with a tone that's mixed with both hope and despair.

"Patrice's fiancé is coming over, so I need your help in preparing dinner and setting the table."

As always, my plans have been interrupted.

"She needs to learn how to cook for him and all those kids she plans to have, and to set the table!" I said. Once again, I really knew how to get the adrenaline flowing at my house.

"Ieshia Sarah Harvey! That mouth of yours . . ."

"Sorry, Mom," I said with a pitiful smirk on my face.

She put her hand on her hip and said, "Change clothes and get back downstairs immediately!"

There you have it! That's my life! I trucked upstairs to my bedroom to change. I changed out of my red, maxi dress. I had cut the bottom of it off because it was too long; Mom and Dad didn't even notice. I put on some cut-off blue jean shorts and an orange t-shirt that I pulled out of the dresser. I knew Mom would not like this look.

I looked again and found a colorful summer dress hanging in the closet. Mom bought it for me last month. I thought it was ugly, but she liked it. Our taste buds of fashion were different, but she was the boss. I grabbed the dress and yanked it over my head.

That's better, I said to myself as I looked in the mirror. Before I headed back downstairs, I wanted to call my boyfriend, Demarcus Andre' Jones. I clicked the digits to call my Boo Thang, and the phone rang.

"Dre'," I said soft and sexy.

"What up, Bae?"

I reply, "I can't come over today."

"Why, Boo?" He replied.

I began to explain my dilemma. "I have to help in the kitchen. Patrice's fiancé is coming over."

"Holla back later," Dre' said.

I hung up the phone. Of course, no one at my house liked Dre'. He was 16, like me, and really cool. I couldn't officially go out on dates yet, so I sometimes snuck off to see him on the weekends.

He was six feet tall, brown skinned, with dreads. His mom was a single parent and worked all the time. His dad was incarcerated. When Dre' was born, his dad held up a local bank, so he was still doing time for that. Dre' didn't go to church, but I liked him. He rapped, sang, and took care of his siblings while his mom worked.

He loved my dance moves!

Dad said we were unequally yoked.

I headed back downstairs in my summer dress. "I am here!" I announced with a smile. "Ieshia Sarah Harvey is here!"

Mom was busy, busy, busy. She was always doing something. "Ieshia, set the table—plates, napkins, forks, spoons, knives, and glasses. Set it for six."

"Who else is coming?"

"Ieshia, work. Stop talking."

"That's kinda hard for me to do!" My mouth blurted out. "But I will try! Love you, Mom!" I gave her a big kiss.

She knew she loved me.

The wood oak table in the dining room was set. I used our best china.

David and Patrice arrive, and Dad came out of the living room with his Sunday afternoon gear on. Suspenders, black slacks, a white long-sleeved shirt, and cuff links. He pulled his burgundy tie off when we got home from church earlier.

Dinner was served. Collard greens, macaroni and cheese, baked ham, mashed potatoes, butter beans, and cornbread, not to mention the red velvet cake and sweet potato pie.

We said grace and ate up.

"Mrs. Harvey," David started his usual round of trying to impress Mom and Dad. "This food is delicious! I have the best future mother-in-law in the world. I thank God for you, and Bishop Harvey too."

"Thank you, David," Mom replied. Mom loved that sweet talk, and Dad loved that Jesus talk.

I rolled my eyes.

"Bishop Harvey," David was still at it. "Blah, blah, blah, blah." That's was all I heard. "Blah, blah, blah. That was a winning sermon today. Blah, blah, blah. 100 years and God is still good! I have some big shoes to fill."

"Son, I appreciate that," Dad said. "When we finish dinner, I will show you where I keep my collection of sermons and how I prepare for worship each Sunday."

David and Patrice have been dating for three and a half years. After high school, David joined the Army and served on Active Duty for three years. He was now in the Army Reserves and served as the full-time Youth Pastor at the church. He did a really good job at working with the youth. The church ran an after school program and weekly youth worship service on Sunday nights. David pretty much kept it going.

The church was getting ready to open a daycare, and Patrice was going to be the director. She had an Associate Degree in Early Childhood Care and Education. She loved children and had been a Sunday School teacher forever. She really was qualified for the job, besides just being Bishop's daughter.

Patrice and David started dating in high school and that's when she made up her mind, he was the one. I think she should have dated around while David was in the Army, but it's always just been her and David. Their wedding was in three months.

I was not going to be working at the church when I graduated from high school. I was going far, far away from all of them.

David interrupted my thoughts again. "Mrs. Harvey, I would love to have another piece of that red velvet cake. It's my favorite." Patrice got up from the table to slice him another piece.

We finished eating just in time for the Coopers to arrive. They stopped by every Sunday to eat with their five kids. Mom said it was better to give than receive, but good grief. Stay home!

Mom went to the door and David gave me a strange look. He freaky! If they only knew. I picked up on people's spirits quick. I had the gift of discernment, as Dad would say. Still do.

The Coopers and their five kids ate all of our leftovers and finally went home. David finally left too. Now, maybe I could make it up to my room for some rest and relaxation. I entered my room and changed into some lounge wear—camo stretch pants and a red tank top. I felt so much better. I twirled around like I was at a dance competition.

I laid across my bed.

Wait. Let me turn my light off and turn the lamp on, so they will think I'm asleep.

I laughed and grabbed my phone to call my Boo back. I dialed Dre's number, but it took him a long time to answer.

I almost hung up, but he finally picked up.

With excitement I said, "Hey, Bae!"

Dre' replied, "What's up?"

"I missed you today. Is your mom home from work yet?"

Dre's sexy voice said, "Nope. She had to pull a double at the carpet factory."

Destin and Dexter, Dre's six-year-old twin sister and brother, were sleep.

"You comin' over?" He asked with a chuckle.

He knew me all too well. I sat up on the bed and said, "You know my rule? I don't come over after 8 p.m."

Dre' sighed and said, "Okay. I am used to seeing you every weekend, Sarah."

"Don't trip," I said. I hated my middle name. It's biblical. Sarah was the "mother of the faithful" in the Holy Bible. "Maybe tomorrow after school."

"Did David give you that look again?"

"Yes, he did."

Dre' got upset and said, "Do you need me to handle it for you?"

"No, Dre'. I don't want you in prison too."

Dre' finally chilled and said, "Let me know and I will cap him."

Dre' got some of his Dad's street ways in him.

His mom never remarried. She was independent and worked all the time. She did have a short rendezvous with a guy that left her with a set of twins, but he paid child support.

Dre' was practically a dad to the twins, and they loved him to life.

Being with Dre' was my release from the world of church and all the Jesus talk. I was my own person, and no one would stop me from seeing him. We said our goodbyes and I hung up the phone.

I turned on some music and started to dance. I danced, and danced, and danced, and danced, and danced.

I envisioned being on stage in front of an audience dancing and leaping in the air. I was the opening act for the American Dance Company, Ieshia Sarah Harvey. The curtains opened and there I was, dancing away, accompanied by Dre'. I leapt into the air and Dre' caught me. We were a great team. Just wait. We were going to do big things.

Before I fell asleep, I said a small prayer to Jesus. Lord, thank You for all you do. Amen.

• • •

Back in the present day, everything looks the same as it did ten years ago. The front porch still has the red swing and navy-blue patio furniture that belongs on a backyard patio and not a front porch. The squeaky banister at the bottom of the stairs still needs fixing.

Dad still never likes to use the fireplace in the living room. He always said Santa Claus could not come down the chimney at Christmas time if we had a fire going. Did he really think we were going to fall for that?

Mom's favorite color was blue, and for as long as I can remember blue has covered the kitchen and bathroom. There is a blue canister set with colorful flowers in the kitchen. There are blue towels in the restroom along with a blue shower curtain. Even the walls are a shade of blue.

As I walk back to the living room, I see my high school picture from 11th grade. Wow! They didn't completely throw me away! I am on the Harvey photo wall of fame. I am shocked.

Mom was a college graduate. She earned her bachelor's degree in Business Administration, but after marrying Dad she became a stay-at-home mom. She's still got mad business sense though, and she puts it to good use.

Mom is over the volunteer ministry at the church and also serves as the director of the homeless shelter the church sponsors. She does a spectacular job leading the staff at the homeless shelter. She partners with several entities that provide job training, mental health counseling, and clothes for the homeless.

Several of the clients that have come through the shelter have transitioned back into a normal way of life, with both a job and a secure home. They often come back to help others and share their stories. Mom's staff really go to bat for her and get the job done. It's a beneficial cause.

Oh, wait! I cannot believe what I'm seeing now! Mom has Malcolm's baby picture up on the wall beside my picture! He was only one year old when I took him to K-mart to get those pictures made. I was so young, but so in love with my toddler son.

Okay! I can do this! I tell myself. Why did Dad head to his office as soon as I arrived?

Lord, help me through this. It has to get better. I am wiser, older, and have my own voice as a single parent and a dance studio owner. My mouth is nothing like it was years ago, but I am still very blunt and outspoken.

Malcolm and I are here for now, but not long. We won't stay after I find somewhere for us to live. In Atlanta, I was the owner of Dancin' in the Rain Dance Studio. We had a two-bedroom apartment below the business.

Malcolm comes into the living room with a gigantic smile on his face.

"Mom," he says.

"Yes, Malcolm?" I reply.

"I really am glad you decided to come back to your home where you grew up. I really think I am going to like it here. I can actually go outside and play in the yard!"

He melts my heart. Smiling, I say, "We have to get you enrolled in school soon."

Malcolm frowns. "Mom. It's the summertime. Can't we wait?"

"No, Malcolm. I am going to the local school board office on Monday morning."

He has no clue why I left home all those years ago or what actually happened. I will tell him one day. For now, I just want him safe and free from harm. He is my child and I have always done right by him. I always will.

The Transition

Chapter 2

Everything had been going well. My dance studio was open for about five years. I had clientele and a staff of three. We all worked hard to teach a variety of dance classes: Hip Hop, Ballet, African, Liturgical, and Creative Movement. Aunt Velma worked as my part-time Office Manager.

My dance studio hosted a recital quarterly. I lived in the heart of Atlanta near some of the city schools and a local community college. Many middle and high school students came after school to dance class. I even partnered with the local college for dance major students to come to work as interns. They were able to share some of their creativity, and the studio was able to serve more students.

I also held morning classes for elderly people who needed to get out of the house and exercise. We brought out music from their younger years and let them have at it. A group of homeschool students would also come to the studio after lunch for a private class.

I never attended college. It wasn't for me. I chose a different path. I was a single mom full of talent, and opportunity was plenty. Plus, I had a great high school dance teacher who gave me everything I needed to run my own studio.

Liturgical dance from my childhood and young teenage years also paid off. When I was fourteen, I started volunteering with the little kids at church teaching liturgical dance along with the Dance Ministry Director. I got that liturgical and ballet dance skill down. I learned my other dance skills, Hip Hop and African, from school and the streets. Most of my training has not been formal. I had natural talent. Still do.

I have been dancing all my life. Mom once told me that when I was around age three, I would dance in the aisles at church. Both at home and at daycare, I drew the attention of others by dancing. It's my gift from God.

I was living my dream life as a Dance Director in Atlanta, but I would seasonally get behind on my mortgage. The studio was my sole income. The high school I attended partnered with me to provide an after school dance program.

They gave me a grant that paid for fifty percent of the students who participated in the program. When the grant ended, the funds disappeared. Some students could pay and continued to come to class, but most could not afford it. I never could turn any students away. I guess part of the "it's better to give than receive" principal I learned from Mom. The kids were dedicated dancers and I wanted to nurture their skills. We were open four days a week and every weekend on Saturday.

About six months ago, a major industry wanted to buy out the block where my studio was. The company planned to build industrial business offices and "gentrify" the area. With my late mortgage payments, it was pretty obvious what I had to do. I signed the papers to sell my place and closed the studio.

Malcolm and I moved back in with Aunt Velma for a short while. Then, the Lord prompted me to return home. Aunt Velma advised me to stay in Atlanta, but with the studio gone, I felt like nothing was holding me there. I love Aunt Velma, and she meant well, but I had no child support and a limited income.

I tried working a couple of temporary office jobs. I tried working as a paraprofessional at a charter academy. I tried sales at a local clothing store. I tried work as a bank teller at Central Bank, but nothing was like my passion for teaching dance.

I recently ended a two-year relationship with Phillip Adams. Elder Adams was his public name, but "on the down low" was his game. He never pressured me about sex because I had vowed not to have sex again until marriage. He knew that from the beginning. Not pressuring me was a good thing, but there was always something strange about him.

My Aunt Velma liked him, and Malcolm really enjoyed his company. We spent a lot of time together and we even traveled. He was very supportive of me with the Dance Studio, but my gut always said something different was going on than what he displayed. He was the owner of a gym called GetFit. Despite my gut saying he wasn't the one, I continued in the relationship because I enjoyed his company and it was better than being alone.

About a month ago, he was supposed to . . . Well, he told me he was going out of town for the weekend on a business trip. Something about job training on new gym guidelines. Before the words came out of his mouth, I knew he was lying, but I went along with it. That weekend, I woke up early and something in my spirit led me to go to his place.

I dressed and slipped out of the house early Saturday morning. When I arrived at his home, I parked a block away. I am really good at going unseen, you know. I used to sneak out of the house when I was younger. I walked near his front yard and saw two vehicles. He had not gone anywhere.

It was still quite early, so I quietly walked up to the front door to peek in through the beveled glass. He had a house guest, and it was not a female. They were sharing an intimate hug on the couch. I immediately bolted, but he heard me. He came to the door as I ran back to my car.

Elder Adams came to the studio that Monday. I was there picking up the last of the things I had left after closing the place. I told him it was over between us, and that he should have come clean with his dating preferences.

He said we could still make it work.

I asked how.

He basically wanted to use me as a cover up for his alternative lifestyle.

Not this chick.

The next month, he was dating his high school sweetheart at the church we attended, and they quickly became engaged. He never could look me straight in the eye again.

Best wishes to him, his fiancé', and his secret lover.

Aunt Velma and Malcolm wondered what happened, but I would never expose him. I am bigger than that. I just told them we had some differences we could not get past and we went our separate ways.

Trust me, men are at me all the time, but I am very picky. I want a husband, but my focus is my son and starting my life over. I don't date a lot because I am a single parent and do not want to bring a variety of men around my son. Before Elder Adams, I did date a country boy named Bob Daniels. He was a construction worker and did carpentry work as a side job on the weekends. He could fix anything and took care all of my repairs at the dance studio. My Aunt Velma introduced me to him because she was really good friends with his mom.

Bob! Oh, Bob! He was raised by his dad in South Georgia after his parents divorced when he was seven. After he graduated from high school, he came to stay with his mom in Atlanta. He wore overalls all the time and always shouted at church. Atlanta did nothing for him; he needed to go back to Brunswick.

He was really cute though, and very mannerable. He always had money and he treated me like a queen. It was fun while it lasted, but I just was not that into him. I admit he had some great qualities, but he never really understood me.

Bob really, really reminded me of Dad. He was over the evangelistic ministry at his church, and always wanted to lead someone to Christ. I was not feelin' it.

In fact, he wanted to lead me to Jesus all of the time. I told him I was already a Christian and I was down with Jesus. He continued to quote scriptures on our dates. It did not matter if we were walking underground Atlanta or shopping at the mall.

I told him he needed to loosen up a little and enjoy life. He worked all the time and evangelized even more. I finally told him it was over, and his response was "Let's pray about it."

Aunt Velma said he was the one for me. I told her he was the one for Jesus.

• • •

A knock at the door brings me back into reality from my not so distant memories of my adult life in Atlanta. I would know that knock anywhere. It is Lady Patrice, and I am about to meet her tribe of four kids. I always knew she was going to have a large family. That was another thing I didn't want—a lot of kids.

Patrice miscarried at two months during her first pregnancy. It was really rough for her, but she got through it with the help of her husband, Pastor David Sanders. That's right, my brother-in-law is now the Associate Pastor at Faith Tabernacle Missionary Baptist Church. One year after her miscarriage, they started having babies: the twins Alexis and Aubrey, David Jr, and Saint Paul. The twins are now 8, David Jr. is 7, and Paul is 6.

Malcolm answers the door. "Hey, Aunt Patrice. I am your nephew, Malcolm."

Lady Patrice picks him up, cries, and hugs him. Her children are going everywhere. She always was the nice one in the bunch. Crack that whoop, I say.

Then she saw me. It was like the scene in *The Color Purple* when Celie and Nettie were united with their sister after many years of separation.

I remember the last time I saw Patrice. She was crying because I was leaving home to go stay with Aunt Velma. I take a deep breath, hug her really hard, and we both cry. What a family reunion! I finally have the opportunity to meet all of her children—my nieces and nephews.

We go downstairs to sit in the living room and talk for hours, like old times. The children go outside in the backyard to play. I am glad Mom and Dad replaced the old swing set we had growing up. I am surprised they did, since Dad is so frugal with his money. Malcolm is showing his cousins his dance moves. They are amazed at him and all seemed to bond.

Patrice is still the daycare director at the church, but now they have two locations. She asks if I would be interested in coming down to teach dance at the daycare. I tell her I will consider it, but she has to pay me. We both laugh.

"David said to tell you hello," she says.

I sigh.

"Why did you not ever like David? He is good to me and the kids. You always looked at him strange when he came around."

I take a deep breath, thinking of how I can avoid the David question when Dad comes into the room.

"Patrice."

"Hey, Dad."

"How are you doing girl?" Dad loves to hug and kiss. He has always been gentle and kind, but he will crack the whoop when he needs too.

I remember one-time Patrice and I were running in the house and we both fell down the stairs and bruised our heads. Dad bruised our butt with that belt and we never ran in the house again.

Dad takes a seat in the recliner, turns to me, and says, "Have you seen or heard from Demarcus? Malcolm's Dad?"

"Dad, now is not a good time."

"He abandoned you and your son," Dad says abruptly. "You should take him to court for back child support. Its time. I will get you a really good lawyer."

"Stop it. I am 26 years old and I am not doing what you tell me. It's not like that. He did write to me a couple of times, but I have not talked to him in years."

"You know," Dad continues, "the strange thing is that he always said Malcolm was not his baby, but he was the only one you were seeing at that time. That never made any sense. I finally let him be since he was young, and his mom was a single parent."

"Dad." I say briskly.

"Ieshia."

I sigh and gasp abruptly. My words are caught in my throat and I feel like I cannot speak.

"Okay," he says. "I will let it be for now. I want my grandson to have the best of the best. Let's put him in the Ivy League Charter Academy."

"DAD! NO! You are not in control of my son's life. I am! I make the decisions. He is my son. Remember, you shipped me off on a bus ten years ago. Why would I entrust in you with directing the well-being of my son?"

"That's enough from both of you." Mom, the boss, walks in on the arguing. Mom never liked to hear us argue. I knew what was coming. Patrice starts crying. Dad leaves the room. Mom goes to comfort him.

Patrice gives me a big hug and whispers, "Why didn't you tell me back then that you were pregnant?"

"Now is not a good time," I say.

Patrice backs up and heads outside to gather her children from the backyard so they can go home. I go to my old bedroom and dance away, just like I used to. It's the only way I know how to deal with the tension and anxiety I feel.

Malcolm knocks at the door, comes in, and asks me to come outside with him. We go back downstairs.

We go to the front yard, stand on the sidewalk, and dance the night away. He is really talented and has some mad skills!

The News

Chapter 3

The alarm clock on my cell phone went off. It was 6 a.m. on Monday morning—time for school again. I got up and dressed while listening to *Black and Yellow* by Wiz Khalifa. I grabbed my book bag and hit the stairs to catch the bus.

I never liked Mom and Dad to drive me to school, so that stopped once Patrice graduated from high school about four years earlier when I was twelve. I was done with car rides to school. They already let me ride the bus occasionally before that, but it became official once they were no longer driving Patrice.

I liked to socialize and ride "the big yellow cheese" school bus. I checked my calendar because my cycle had still not come. It's been over a month since I should have started. If I told mom, she was going to think I was pregnant.

If I told Patrice, she would think it would ruin her wedding. I was one of her seven bridesmaids. Yes, she was planning a very large wedding, and Dad was paying for it. He did give her a budget though.

Well, I can't tell Dre.' I thought. He would think I have cheated, and I am not even sleeping with him. He wanted some, but I kept it clean and holy.

Mr. Mill, the bus driver, pulled up at the bus stop near the corner of our house. I got on the bus with the other kids from the neighborhood and said, "Good morning, Mr. Mills."

Mr. Mills was a Vietnam War Veteran. He served in the Marine Corp for fifteen years and received an honorable discharge. He drove the bus to give back to the community, but he also owned a local grocery store.

"Good morning, Ieshia," Mr. Mills replied as he started slowly driving to the next stop in the neighborhood. "I see you are ready for school."

"That's right. Let's get it started." I danced down the bus aisle to the back and sat with Dre'. We crank up our music.

I was in the 10th grade and had a ton of friends. School was pretty dope. I acted like I never paid attention in class, but I still managed to pass with A's and B's. I was a really good listener and I read my textbooks and notes at home.

As we were getting off the bus, Dre' asked me if I was ready for the math test.

"Math test? What test?" I shouted and grabbed my head. After the church anniversary this weekend and entertaining the Cooper kids, I was swamped and had forgotten all about it.

We went on to breakfast in the lunchroom. While everyone else ate the dry toast, hard bacon, and watery grits, I pulled out my notes and begin to review for the Geometry exam.

The bell rang and we were dismissed to go to homeroom, our first block class. I should have eaten something before leaving home this morning, or at least in the cafeteria, but I didn't. My brain was on music, friends, and then the test.

I hated tests, but I was good at them. Once again, I managed to pull it off with an 85 on the exam. I was usually an A student and should have been in accelerated classes, but I just didn't feel like pushing myself. Class was really easy for me, but I would never tell anyone that! I thought if my teachers knew my potential, they would challenge me all of the time.

I made it through my other classes and finally to lunchtime. I pulled out my ear buds and listened to my playlist during lunch. Lunch was horrible. Since Mrs. Allen, the Head Cook, retired, lunch was not the same. She was the main cook for 30 years, and everybody loved her. She could care less about the nutrition guidelines set by the government. Her food was seasoned, and she always put extra on everybody's plate, especially mine. I missed her smiling face.

I grabbed an apple off of Dre's tray, ate it, and drank a bottle of water. That would have to do. It was time for dance class—my favorite—with Mrs. Reeves. She attended New York University for the Arts and landed a job in Georgia. She was originally from Charleston, South Carolina, and had family in Georgia, so it was a good fit. Her accent was all over the place, but she knew her stuff. I absolutely loved her class. I was her top-notch student. She wanted me to get involved with the band dance line, but Dad wouldn't allow me to even try out.

As we finished up with class, Mrs. Reeves turned to me. "Ieshia, great job today in class."

"Thanks, Mrs. Reeves." I gave her a really big Kool-Aid smile as I stood tall with pride. We were rehearing for our upcoming recital at the St. Patrick's Day Festival we performed at every year. I normally had a solo performance.

"Ieshia?"

"Yes, ma'am?"

"Ieshia! Are you okay?"

I didn't even know what happened, but later they told me I passed out. Mrs. Reeves buzzed the main office and they sent the school nurse down to the classroom.

I was unresponsive, so they call for the ambulance. I heard them calling my name, but I couldn't say anything. The paramedics arrived and I don't remember anything else. I woke up in the hospital attached to an IV.

Mom was there and she started crying.

I was lying in the hospital bed just waking up from my daze.

Mom stood by the bed and said, "Why didn't you tell us?"

"What are you talking about?" I said with a puzzled look on my face. "Tell you what?"

Mom's face tightened up and she gave me her look.

"Don't lie to me."

Again, I said, "What are you talking about? I am in the hospital. What happened?"

I began to rewind my day in my mind and tried to remember what had taken place that morning. I went to school like I always did. I had a math test. I didn't skip class. What the what?

Mom gave me that look again. She was so frustrated. "IESHIA SARAH HARVEY, YOU ARE SIX WEEKS PREGNANT!"

I became defensive and said, "Who told you that? What are you talking about? I am not pregnant."

Nothing was making sense. I sat up in the hospital bed. I had a momentary flashback, grabbed my head, and laid back down.

Dr. Larry Johns, the resident MD, walked in.

"Good afternoon Ieshia. How are you feeling? Do you remember what happened?"

He full of questions and cute too.

I began to speak. "Dr. Johns, I was in dance class at school and about to wrap it up and then that's it."

Mom rudely interrupted, her hand on her hip notating her seriousness.

"The school secretary called and said she had passed out. While I was in route to the school, Nurse Andrews called back and said they had an ambulance go pick her up, so I turned around and began to head to the hospital instead."

Dr. Johns started talking again, sparing me the details of Mom's drive.

"We drew some blood and ran some tests. Ieshia, you are six weeks pregnant. You passed out because you had not eaten. You have low blood sugar and your blood pressure was elevated. You will need to start taking prenatal vitamins immediately. Eat three times a day and keep some snacks with you at all times."

My eyes widened, and I became numb. "Doc, I watch my weight. I am a dancer."

Mom chimed in again, "She will eat, Dr. Johns. Ieshia! What am I going to tell your Dad? How could you?"

"But, Mom . . ."

"Hush!"

"I am referring her to a gynecologist for a follow-up appointment," Dr. Johns said. "My staff nurse set up an appointment for Wednesday morning at 9 a.m. For now, she can go home. Nurse Taylor will come up with the discharge papers."

Nurse Taylor attended our church. She was really messy, and I wondered who she had already called to blab my personal business to. Nurse Taylor shook her head while we signed the discharge papers. *For shame!*

I get dressed, grab my things, and go home with Mom. It was the longest ride home ever. Mom didn't even turn on her gospel music. She just cried and shook her head. She already called Dad. He was making some kind of arrangements, but I didn't know what at the time.

I could sense in my spirit what would happen. I was not having an abortion. I was keeping my baby. I took a deep breath and rested my head on the seat in the car. My world was flipping upside down.

We got home and I immediately went to my room. I opened the door, entered my bedroom, threw my book bag on the floor, and sat down at my desk. I wanted to scream but couldn't. I took my cellphone out of my purse. I needed to talk to somebody—NOW. I started going through my phone contacts. All my friends were at school.

Patrice was at the church preparing for the daycare's grand opening. Did she even know what was going on?

Dre'. . . I couldn't call him.

Who knew I was pregnant? God did.

Lord, I really need you here. Pregnant?

I started having flashbacks. I screamed.

Mom ran in the room and held me. She wiped my tears.

I started silently reassuring myself.

I am a Harvey. I will survive. The Greater One lives inside of me.

Scripture sure will rise up in you when you need it!

Mom stood up from sitting with me on the bed and said, "Your dad wants to see you in the study."

I took a deep breath and said softly, "Yes, ma'am."

Mom and I went back downstairs to Dad's office and we all sat down. The study was rather large. He had a small conference table in there, but we sat opposite of him at his desk. He was always dressed in suit and tie, sitting at his chestnut oak desk with his Bible open. He took his glasses off.

Here we go.

He sat up in his chair and said, "Ieshia, you are 16-years-old and too young to be having sex. I raised you better than that. You and Patrice vowed to practice abstinence until marriage. Where did I go wrong with you?"

"Dad . . ."

"Hush! I can't have this right now. We are getting ready to open the daycare and your sister's wedding is in three months. I have no choice. You are going to live with your Aunt Velma in Atlanta."

"But, Dad," I said with tears in my eyes. "Let me explain." I started crying.

"I have already called her, and you will take the Greyhound in the morning. Your mother will withdraw you from school and transfer temporary guardianship to your aunt. We will send money to support you and the baby."

"But, Dad!" I was crying. "Let me explain, please."

Dad said, "There is nothing to explain. You have been having sex with Demarcus Andre' Jones. I have already called his mom and updated her."

Again, I tried again to tell my side. "Dad! You control everything!"

"Shut up and get out of my office."

I stood up and looked at Mom.

"Mom, say something," I begged.

She was just sitting there in tears.

I left his office and slammed the door. I stormed up the stairs and went back to my room. I was so angry, I started to pack throwing clothes violently into my bag.

I started talking to myself again.

I can do this. I need a fresh start.

But then the flashbacks started again, and I panicked and started crying.

Mom came in to help me pack. After we finished, I went to bed angry and in tears.

Early the next morning, I woke up and got dressed. As I walked out of my room with my luggage, Patrice came out of her bedroom and grabbed me.

"I love you," she whispered in my right ear.

Gosh, Patrice need to work on her morning breath before saying "I Do . . ."

Dad didn't even say good-bye.

Mom and I walked through the kitchen to the side door that led into the garage. Mom popped open the trunk and I loaded in my luggage. She drove me to the Greyhound station, but we stopped at McDonald's first. I got a chicken sandwich with juice and a side order of fruit.

Luckily, Mom and Dad had already set me up with a checking account at the local bank when I was 12 years old. I had a little bit of my own money saved. I knew Dad would wire money to Aunt Velma.

He won't put it in my account, even though he loaded with money.

We arrived at the bus station. Mom parked and got out of the car. We unloaded my luggage and rolled up to the ticket counter.

Mom gave me the ticket and put some money in my hand. She gave me a big hug. She cried again and said, "I will be calling to check on you. I will email you weekly."

She grabbed my shoulders and looked into my eyes with love, compassion, and pain.

"I know you are upset with us, but sending you away was Dad's plan—not mine. It hurts me to put you on this bus, but I have to honor your Dad's wishes."

I boarded the bus and sat down beside an older Hispanic lady. She may be around 50 years old. She was cold and abrupt. Who knows what her issue was? I tried not to judge. I accepted her where she was at. I waved good-bye out the window to Mom from my seat.

I had always been the black sheep of the family. I never did what I was told and hated being a preacher's kid. I began to cry. I cried, cried, cried. It was all coming out. Nothing was making sense. I had the window seat on the bus, so I leaned my head on the glass. It was now good and wet with my tears, almost baptism style. I felt so numb, trying to make sense of it all.

I finally fell asleep. I had my ear buds in listening to one of Dad's sermons I recorded with my phone. I dreamt I was dancing, pregnant. I twirled in a pink ruffle dress with pink ballerina shoes on.

"Senorita?" The Hispanic lady nudged me awake.

She was short and had very pretty long black hair.

I wonder if can she dance? What's her story?

"We are here," she said.

I yawned, stretched my arms, and stood up. When I got off the bus, I saw Aunt Velma. She was like a second mom to me. The Greyhound bus driver unloaded the luggage from the bottom of the bus. I grabbed my navy-blue suitcases.

Aunt Velma gave me a big hug and said, "It's going to be okay. I got you. We will get through this together."

That's what Mom and Dad should have been saying.

Aunt Velma was a widow. Her husband died of prostate cancer five years ago. He was a corporate lawyer and they had been married for twenty-eight years. They never had any children. The bus driver graciously loaded my three suitcases into the trunk of Aunt Velma's BMW. We got in, strapped up, and started the drive to her house.

Aunt Velma was wealthy, but very humble. Uncle Ricky left her a nice insurance policy along with his investments and savings accounts. She had a very large home, five bedrooms, four bathrooms, a living room, dining room, kitchen, two offices, a basement, and a pool.

Once we entered her home, she said to me, "Go unpack. Rest and come back down later for dinner."

"Yes, ma'am."

She escorted me to my new bedroom—the largest guest bedroom in the house.

Since I was pregnant, she gave me the downstairs room. I had my own bathroom, with an adjoined office connected to the bedroom. The room was large. It had a door that led to the back patio.

Aunt Velma is living large.

She hugged me again and gave me a really big kiss on the cheek before she left the room, closing the door behind her.

I took another deep breath as I looked around. How much more could I bear?

I closed my eyes and tried to sing a song. That didn't work. I had to pee, again. Now it made sense why I've been peeing a lot lately.

I got up, used the restroom, flushed the toilet, and washed my hands. After drying my hands, I looked in the mirror.

Six weeks pregnant?

I pulled up my shirt and took a good look at my stomach.

A baby is in me? That's why my cycle skipped a month.

My life would never be the same. It was different from this point on. I needed to pick out a name. I sat on the queen-sized bed and I grabbed a Bible from the nightstand.

I begin to read Psalm 23. It's was comforting to me. In my mind, I could hear Patrice singing the 23rd Psalm with her middle school choir.

I stood up to dance, but I couldn't. My fire was gone.

What is happening to me?

I started crying again and fell across the bed in anguished distress.

Wait! I am Ieshia Sarah Harvey! How could they just ship me off?

Okay. It is not time to play the blame game, I argue with myself.

I had an opportunity for a fresh start. A transition. I wasn't that happy with my life at home. Maybe this could be a good thing. Change comes and we must adjust. I laid back down on the bed and fell fast asleep.

After I awoke from my nap, I made another trip to the restroom. That sleep was good and there was a slobbery stain on the side of my mouth to prove it. I washed my face and took a deep breath.

I walked down the hall to the kitchen to have dinner with Aunt Velma.

Her kitchen is huge.

She and Uncle Ricky did a lot of entertaining when he was alive and in good health. Office parties, Christmas, and New Years' Eve get-togethers.

They even had a housemaid, Ms. Joiner. She still came to clean for Aunt Velma, but not as much as before Uncle

Ricky died. Instead of coming daily, she came twice a week now. Aunt Velma's gardener, Pedro, still came to cut the grass and trim the trees.

We ate brown rice, baked chicken, and mixed vegetables. Aunt Velma did not cook like Mom, but it would do.

I knew she was wondering what is going on. No one knew my truth. After dinner, we sat on the back patio, relaxed, listening to Jazz music, and then went to bed.

Aunt Velma was and is very different from Dad, even though they are brother and sister. She drank wine and a little Hennessey in her soft drinks. She also liked to dance. She laughed and told me stories of growing up in Dublin with Dad and their other siblings. Aunt Velma even smoked, but she told me she would stop since I was pregnant.

The next day, Aunt Velma and I travel to the Hinesville Academy School of Art and Dance—a prestigious private school. She was on the board of directors. The students wear uniforms.

It was going to be different, but I told myself, "I got this." I was determined to keep a positive attitude.

Uncharted Territory

Chapter 4

It's Sunday morning at Mom and Dad's and the sun is bright outside. The birds are chirping away.

I remember dreading getting out of this bed as a child and teenager because I knew it would be a full day at Faith Tabernacle Missionary Baptist Church. As a kid, I used to go to sleep in church and Mom would pop me to wake me up. They started children's church when I was in high school, so as a child I missed the opportunity to get the word on my level.

Now it's different. I anticipate getting up on Sundays and every day. God has been good to me. I recognize and clearly see my role in life. I do not have any regrets. I eagerly climb out of bed. I can't wait to hear Dad preach today.

Dad had been preaching since I was in Mom's womb. Growing up as a PK, it felt like nobody knew our truth. We had a normal life, Mom made sure of that, but we were held to a higher standard.

I wake up before everyone else. I rinse off my face, brush my teeth, tiptoe downstairs, and enter the kitchen. Oh, the memories! Upon closer inspection, it looks like they *have* remodeled *some*. I see a new stove and microwave. The kitchen table has been re-stained. Is that a new sink? Wow.

I start breakfast. I even turn on a little gospel music from our local radio station. They are playing Marvin Sapp.

While I am in the kitchen, Malcolm wakes up and checks my bedroom. He comes downstairs and tries to scare me. He is such a clown.

Just like Mom would do to me, I put him to work. He actually enjoys it. He learned at an early age how to help his mother in the kitchen. My thinking was that, yes, he is going to be someone's husband one day, but he has to know how to fend for himself during his bachelor season first.

Everyone wakes up to the aroma coming from the kitchen. The family all come down the stairs in their housecoats to eat. Mom is tickled pink.

"All those times you didn't want to help me in the kitchen, but it paid off," she said.

I smile and give her a kiss, as I did growing up.

Breakfast is served: cheese grits, turkey bacon, sausage balls, scrambled eggs, biscuits, and apple juice. I also made a breakfast casserole.

Malcolm volunteers to say grace. His morning prayers are much better than mine were when I was his age. We join hands as Malcolm prays.

"Dear Father, thank You for this day. I am so glad to be at my mom's house. Thank You for this food we are about to receive. In Jesus' name we pray . . ."

And everyone said, "Amen."

While we eat up, Malcolm has tons of questions for Dad. Dad cackles away and answers them. Mom is still as busy as a bee.

"Mom, you can go on and get ready for church. Malcolm and I will clean the kitchen."

She rushes upstairs to get dressed. Malcolm, of course, eats the leftovers from breakfast as he helps me load dishes into the dishwasher. He wipes off the table for me, and we go back upstairs to get dressed for church.

We come downstairs and load up in the SUV. Dad finally upgraded from that Black Cadillac. As always, Dad has to do the traveling prayer. He wasn't taking any chances with me, so he asked Mom to pray.

I chuckle and Mom just smiles.

Mom and Dad live about fifteen minutes from the church. Malcolm is beaming with excitement and hugs his cousins as they proceed to the children church classroom in the back, while the rest of us attend Adult Sunday School. Sister Magnolia Mae is still teaching with her hat on. It seems to me that she knows every line of the Bible.

They have expanded the church some since I left. They added classrooms and opened up a large room for the youth to have church in. It seats 100 kids.

After Sunday School, Lady Patrice comes and gives me a big hug before the worship service begins.

The church now even has a praise team! I can't believe it. Faith Tabernacle Missionary Baptist Church has really upgraded and grasped the twentieth century worship style. They incorporate modern day worship with a traditional flavor. While the choir sings, the liturgical dance team comes out.

The church announcements play from a prerecorded video created by the church technology staff. They decided to be cute and call themselves the "Church Report."

Then Dad gets up and introduces the guest speaker.

Guest speaker? I really wanted to hear Dad this morning.

There he is. Front and center—Pastor David Sanders! He looks older. We all have aged, but we still fine. He looks shocked to see me. He takes a deep breath and preaches quite well. Lady Patrice leads a song during altar call. Sis is still bad on that mic! As always, she shouts the house down! Mom stands up to worship as she always did.

Church is over and everybody wants to speak to me and give me hugs. I am actually glad to see everyone. It's good to see old friends and classmates. Is that Demarcus Andre' Jones I see in the crowd? Okay, let me not stare, but I think that may be him.

Everyone remembers me. I now know I did the right thing by coming back home. The Spirit will never lead you wrong.

Patrice invites us to her home to eat Sunday Dinner.

This is going to be interesting.

We go back home to change and then drive to her house. She lives in a new subdivision about fifteen minutes from where Mom and Dad live.

"I like this, Sis," I say to her as we enter her six-bedroom brick home. "You livin' large!"

Each of her children has their own bedroom. They have a pool and can all swim. I am so glad Malcolm learned to swim when he was younger. Still, to for safety, they have a playground area that is fenced, separating it from the pool.

Mom and I help Patrice prepare the dinner table. She whispers to tell us she thinks she is expecting again.

Girl, you better handle that with some tubulation snips or birth control, I think to myself. It can't be healthy for her to keep having so many babies.

She took a home pregnancy test and it came back positive. I told her to go to her OB/GYN quick, fast, and in a hurry.

We all sit down to eat in her dining room. Dad says the prayer. As always, he gets happy and offers up a long prayer. I used to time him when I was younger.

Pastor David Sanders can't even look at me. He attempts to give me a hug, but I pull away. Patrice sees it, but she doesn't say anything. We make it through dinner.

After dinner, David and Dad went to visit some elderly members at the nursing home. Us girls all work together to clean the kitchen, and the kids go out back to play.

"Sis, when are you going to come to the daycare?" Patrice asks.

"Hmm, soon," I say slowly.

Mom says, "I really would like for you to come to the homeless shelter. It has grown so much."

"So y'all tryin' to put me to work already?" I say jokingly. "I am good financially for now. I got a nice settlement with the buyout of the dance studio. I got some stock investments. I learned that from Aunt Velma. You know she loaded and know how to make money."

"Okay," both Mom and Patrice say.

"We are here if you need us," Mom adds.

"I just want to take it slow and go from there. I want to get Malcolm enrolled in school, settled in with that, and then look for a home for us."

Mom says, "Y'all can stay with us until you find work and get re-established." Then she changes the subject. "I kinda agree with Dad . . . What he said the other day at the house. You really need to seek legal counsel regarding childcare payments from Demarcus!"

I have had it!

"He is not the father! Roll off him!" I say firmly with boldness.

The kids come in, sweaty from playing outside. They drink some Gatorade, cool down for a few minutes, and then go back out at it. Some of the neighborhood kids come over to join them.

Patrice asks, "What do you mean Demarcus is not the dad? Girl, you got to let this out and update us."

"What do you mean?" Mom looks shocked. "Y'all had been dating for two years—though you thought we didn't know. What is that supposed to mean? *He is not the father?* Ieshia, what are you not telling us? Something from the story is missing. Is that why he always told Dad the baby was not his?"

"Yes, that's right. I never had sex with him. I was a virgin."

"What?" Mom and Patrice both stand up and then sit back down as Dad and David return from the nursing home and walk into the living room. We never finish the conversation.

We eventually say our goodbyes and head back to Mom and Dad's house. Our bellies are full, but Dad and Malcolm sit on the front porch and manage to eat ice-cream cones filled with chocolate ice-cream and covered with nuts.

Mom and I sit on the back patio to chat.

"Ieshia, I am so confused. Are you sure you did not sleep with Demarcus?"

"Mom, I was sixteen, but far from stupid. I remember very vividly."

Mom grabs my hand and says, "Why didn't you tell me?"

"You never gave me a chance to tell my story. I was shipped off, remember?"

"Ieshia, I am your mother and I demand some answers!"

"Well, I am your daughter. I love you and don't want to disrespect you, but this conversation is over. There is so much y'all do not know."

I give her a kiss and retire to my room for the night.

Malcolm comes in from eating his ice-cream and gives me a big hug. He then heads across the hall to Patrice's old bedroom—his sleeping quarters for now. He hates the silky pink bed comforter set, but it is temporary.

He comes back to my room and asks me if he can go back to Aunt Patrice's house to play tomorrow.

"Boy, get to bed!"

Atlanta

Chapter 5

"Ieshia," the Dean of students, Dr. Thomas greeted me as Aunt Velma, and I walked into his office. We sat down and he continued his introductory speech.

"I am so elated to have you here at our Hinesville Academy Campus. Our school theme is, *Great Expectations: Great Horizons.* That motto produces competent scholars who graduate and go on to attend ivy league schools on full academic or performing arts scholarships.

"Your former high school faxed all your school records over, and our Registrar and School Counselor have reviewed your transcript. You are a high performing student when it comes to tests and have an A average in most of your classes. That's a sign you don't push hard enough."

What the what? I think. *He is reading me, oh, too well.*

"Yes sir, that is correct," I smiled.

"You are academically ahead, and we want to have you tested for our gifted program," he said. "Your classes will be in the morning, and after lunch your enrichment class will be dance. Your aunt, Mrs. London, says you have been dancing since you were a little girl."

"Yes, sir. I have."

Ms. London . . . Aunt Velma . . . I forgot that was her married last name.

Dr. Thomas continues, "Our performing arts program will allow you to develop your fundamental dance and performing skills and enter a dance career pathway before graduating from high school."

A knock at the door interrupted him.

"Come in," Dr. Thomas said.

The woman who entered was wearing nursing scrubs.

"This is Nurse Richards, our school nurse. She is aware that you are pregnant. I want you to go by her office to check in with her every day. I will follow up with her weekly to check on your status."

"Hi, Ieshia. You are in good hands now. I had my first child at 17-years-old. I have been where you are at. Any questions you have, I will answer. Know that you are okay to dance. That will be your exercise.

"I have connected your aunt with a great OB/GYN in the city. She's a female doctor and she will make you feel comfortable. Once you finish your appointments, you can come on back to school."

"Your first appointment is tomorrow morning at 8 a.m.," Aunt Velma added.

I took a deep breath, and graciously said, "Thank you for everything. I am eager to get started with class and especially dance."

Nurse Richards left, and Dean Thomas continued talking.

"We will have you take a tour of the building today and you can officially start classes tomorrow," Dr. Thomas said.

"Thank you, Dean Thomas."

We left his office, and Aunt Velma decided to sit in the lobby while I went on the school tour with the office intern, Kelly. The Academy was huge and nothing like my old high school.

As we walk out of the office, Kelly and I began to talk.

"Where you from?" She asked.

"Dublin."

"I am from Statesboro."

"How did you end up in Atlanta?" I asked.

"My parents were killed in a car accident, so I came up here to live with family."

Wow, I think. Everybody has a story. That has to be rough for her.

I didn't say anything about my story.

Finally, after going up stairs and meeting all of my new teachers, we made it to the dance studio—the only class I really cared about. It was in Wing B adjacent to the theater.

I walked in to meet the dance instructor. She was a white chick, but she could really dance. She was dancing when I entered the room and I was mesmerized.

After she finished her routine, she came over and Kelly introduced us.

"What's up, Ieshia?" Ms. Nichols smiled. "Welcome to Dance Studio 101. It's hot, we make it rain, and you work for what you earn in this class. You ready for the push?"

"Yes, ma'am!" I smiled, feeling at home for the first time in days.

"See you tomorrow."

She was really hip! She reminded me of Debbie Allen from the movie *Fame.* Yes, even as a young girl I was old-school when it came to my favorite movie choices.

Before heading to the car, Aunt Velma and I swung back by the office to sign out. We hopped on the interstate and drove to a shopping plaza.

I needed to shop for uniform-style school clothes. Then we needed to go grocery shopping. Aunt Velma was really cool and seemed to be having a great time. We were both having a great time actually.

She drove me all around Atlanta. It was so different from where I used to live in Dublin. We stopped to eat lunch at a local restaurant downtown. We sat outside at tables the restaurant had out on the sidewalk. The breeze felt good and the music sounded even better.

Appetizer. Entrée. Dessert.

I could get used to this, but it was still not home. I missed my family. I missed Dre'. I missed Patrice.

But, why? I thought. *None of them really know me or what happened.*

The waitress came one final time after we finished eating, and Aunt Velma paid for lunch and gave the girl a tip. The waitress smiled and walked away.

I wondered how much that tip was.

"Are you ready to go?" Aunt Velma asked.

"Yes, ma'am, but let me go to the bathroom first. After I returned to the table, we grabbed our purses and headed to the BMW. On our way to the car, a panhandler approached us.

"Do you have any spare change?" He asked.

Aunt Velma looked into her purse and pulled out a twenty-dollar bill.

"Thank you, Ms. Velma," he responded.

"How do you know him, Aunt Velma?" I asked once we were in the car.

She began to tell his story. "He used to work with your Uncle years ago at the law firm."

"What happened?"

"He was terminated, and his wife left him. He lost everything and ended up on the streets. Your Uncle Ricky and I tried several times to help him, but he refused. Whenever I see him on the street, I always give him money or get him a hot meal."

That was my first time seeing an actual panhandler. It was hard to believe he was someone Aunt Velma knew.

We finally pulled out onto the highway. Aunt Velma was rocking it in her shades and a short purple dress. She was dazzling, both in her charm and clothing. She loved to wear jewelry and bracelets. She didn't talk about the Lord much, but she knew her Redeemer lived.

"Oh, how I miss your Uncle Ricky," she said as she drove. "He was my rock and my heart. Loving him for twenty-eight years was easy because he loved me back. Marriage takes work, but we made it."

"I hated seeing his health decline after his diagnosis and cancer treatment, but I was always going to stick by him until the end. I was right by his side when he died. Life has not been the same since he left, but I have adjusted. Grief is still there in my heart. I even went to counseling."

"Aunt Velma . . . Are you coo-coo?" I gently asked.

"Girl, no! There is such a taboo on African American people about going to counseling. I needed it. It helped me through a troubling time in my life. My home is empty but also filled with many memories of him. I need to do a yard sale."

My light bulb comes on. "Aunt Velma, just donate his clothes to a charity that can distribute his suits to men in need."

"Girl, you are on to something! I will consider that."

I didn't know she could talk the way she did. I was enjoying it. What else did she have to say? I was only 16, still growing, and I had a lot to learn. I wanted to learn it from Aunt Velma.

She started up again. "Girl, when your dad called me, he was in a panic. He is such a control freak. He was like that growing up, but he always had a heart for others. That's why he is such a loving Pastor. I remember when he first met your mom."

"You do?"

"He saw her at a clothing store. We were out shopping for a Mother's Day gift for our mom. He accidentally bumped into her, but I think he did it on purpose. She was really shy, but he was sprung at first sight. He got her number and never looked back.

"When he called me last week, I told him to just let you come stay with me for now and finish high school. Please don't be upset with him. Your mother hated the idea because she really wanted to help with the baby, her first grandchild, and to nurture you as a brand-new mom.

"But, as always, she respects his wishes. That's always been your mom. She loves your dad and will support him, every step of the way."

It was a long ride home, but we finally made it back to the mansion. We unloaded the bags of groceries and my new school clothes. As I helped Aunt Velma put the groceries away, I heard someone outside.

"Aunt Velma, who is that guy?"

"That is Pedro. Pedro!" she called to him.

"Yes, Senorita?"

"Come inside for a moment. He put the garden shears down and walked in through the patio door.

"This is my niece, Ieshia. She is going to be here for a while living with me. She is expecting and I am going to help her raise her child."

"Nice to meet you," he nodded.

"Nice to meet you too."

"Adios!"

Pedro went back outside to finish up the yard.

As Aunt Velma and I take my clothes to my bedroom, I am surprised my bed is made. Startled again, I asked, "Aunt Velma, did you do this?"

She laughed and said, "No, girl. That was my housemaid, Ms. Joiner. She came while we were out."

"You trust her like that?"

"She has been cleaning for me for the past twenty years. Of course, I trust her. Girl, I also got cameras everywhere and an app on my phone so I can see everything that happens here. I don't play. Your dad and I grew up on the southside of Dublin. We 'hood,' for real, and can smell a rat quick.

"Ms. Joiner will iron your clothes. Just be sure to put your dirty clothes in the clothes hamper in your room."

"Okay," I said.

"I am going to go out in the garden to do a little work on my flowers while Pedro is here. You relax, gather your thoughts, and rest in your new home."

"Yes, ma'am," I said. She gave me a big hug before she left to go upstairs to her bedroom to change into her gardening clothes.

I took another deep breath. I decided to walk around her beautiful home to check everything out. I went upstairs to see all of the bedrooms first. Wow, I didn't know she had a pool room up here too.

Aunt Velma was back downstairs and outside, so I decided to take a peek into her bedroom and walk-in closet. I was amazed by all of her clothes. She even had a separate closet for her shoes!

I could really tell there were no kids or grandkids around. It was too clean.

Ha! Ha! Ha! Oh, well. Everybody life's journey is different.

I sensed she was genuine and down for me, no matter what.

Am I prophet? I thought momentarily. *Nope. Not at all.* But I knew she needed me. She was gonna help me, and I was gonna help her. I went back down the stairs and to my room.

I had to use the restroom again. I took off my jeans and t-shirt to throw on some more relaxing clothes. I forgot there was an office area in my room.

I saw a laptop and an iPad on the desk. I really liked that iPad! I brought it back to my bed, synced it to my phone, and pulled up all my music playlists.

Wait! I tell myself. *There is a baby inside of me. I need to be careful what I listen to.*

I downloaded a Bible app and some church stuff, but I didn't delete Drake. He was my favorite, along with Nicki Manji. I was hardcore with my music, but I could also lighten it up as well, for the baby.

I laid there and started to think. My mind seemed overwhelmed in a way that music—for the first time—couldn't sort out.

When I would get into trouble at school, my old school counselor would encourage me. She told me I should write in a journal. I never did anything the School Counselor suggested, but now seemed to be a really good time to start.

Disclosure

Chapter 6

Malcolm is hanging with Mom today at the homeless shelter, so I drop him off there and head to register him for school. I make it to the school board office in Dublin to meet with the Director of Student Services. I register my son for school, but we have to wait for the paperwork to come from his old school before the transfer will be official.

Since its summer, there may be a delay on the paperwork, but Malcolm is set to begin fifth grade in the fall at the local elementary school.

Ms. Berry gives me a list of school supplies and the dress code policy. Being that it is a smaller district, and nothing like he is used to in Atlanta, Malcolm will have to adjust. At least his new school wears uniforms, and he can still wear some of what he wore at the Hinesville Academy. He is growing, so I may have to buy all new clothes regardless.

Everyone at the school board office is really nice. There is nothing like southern hospitality and charm. I did not find that much in Atlanta.

As I walk out of the office, I bump into a man wearing a bow tie.

"Excuse me, ma'am," he said as he pushed his glasses back up the bridge of his nose.

"Good morning, sir."

"I didn't mean to bump you."

"No problem," I say, even though he nearly knocked me down.

I get back into my car, for some reason my mind is stuck on the man from the hall.

He sure is stiff and congested. He too nerdy.

I decide to drive around to see my old hometown. I notice some changes and some things that remain the same.

Is that Dre'? My mind questions as I glance at the driver passing me by on the other side of the road. I wave as I sit at the red traffic light. The other driver waves back, but no it is not Dre'.

Should I call him? No, he has nothing to do with us.

I can definitely tell it is summertime. Kids are on the sidewalk riding their bikes, and parents are walking into stores with their children.

What's next for me? I wonder. God has a plan and I must continue to trust Him. Before I forget, let me swing by the daycare to see Patrice. I pull up and see David outside. I pretend like I don't see him.

I go into the daycare. There are children everywhere. I hear voices, nursery rhymes, and the alphabet song. Patrice loves it, but there is no way I would sign up for this.

The secretary in the lobby knows who I am and gives me the okay to go on back to see Patrice in her office.

"Hey, Sis," I say as I enter and sit down.

She is finishing up a phone call.

"You finally made it."

"Yes, I did."

"Where is Malcolm?"

"He's with Mom today."

"Gotcha. What have you been up to today?"

"You all in my business."

"You still got that mouth, Ieshia."

"Since you want to know my every move, I went to the school board office and got Malcolm registered for school in the fall. I also rode around town. A lot has changed."

"Yes, it has. You feel like talking?" Patrice asks.

"No, I don't."

Her phone rings again. It's the secretary announcing a visitor.

"Send him on back," Patrice says.

"Oh, I can leave," I say, thinking it is David.

"No, Sis please stay."

I sit back down.

"Dr. Stanley! Come on in!" Patrice says warmly.

"So good to see you, Mrs. Sanders."

I look up a bit shocked. It is the same man that almost knocked me over at the School Board office this morning.

"Dr. Stanley, this is my sister, Ieshia Harvey. She has just moved back home from Atlanta."

"Nice to meet you ma'am," he shakes my hand after he shakes Patrice's.

He is so nerdy.

"Thank you for allowing me to come and talk with you today, Ms. Patrice. We love the great things you are doing at your daycare locations. Once again, our school district was awarded a five-year grant and would love to partner with you to provide some enrichment opportunities for our students during after school programs."

"Dr. Stanley, you are a prayer answered. I look forward to working with you again."

"These are some documents for you to review and I will send an email over with more information. Thank you and see you soon."

He gets up to walk out.

"Good day ma'am," he says to me.

After he leaves, I say to Patrice, "He needs a makeover."

"Girl, leave that man alone. He is the School Initiative and Program Director for the local school system. He has been here for about five years."

"Moving on . . ." I say, "What do you want me to do here today?"

"Can you teach my kids some simple dance moves?"

"Sure. My dance bag is in the car."

I go grab my bag and come back inside to change clothes. Some of the students are coming back from lunch.

"Let's go into Ms. Power's classroom," Patrice says.

We walk into the room and Patrice introduces me.

"Class today we have Ms. Harvey with us. Can you say hello?"

"Hello, Ms. Harvey," the class says.

"She is going to do some dancing with you on today before you go to recess."

This should be interesting. I am used to working with older kids, at least age 7, not 3 and 4-year-olds.

"Okay. Let's go! Everybody stand up!" I say as the kids excitedly follow my every move.

It's a wrap and a success. My sister thinks I am going to come every day, but that is so not going to happen. I committed to two days a week for the rest of this summer only.

After I leave the daycare, I drive to the homeless shelter to pick up Malcolm. He is having a ball showing some of the men how to dance. He might be on to something. Aunt Velma taught us well, because of her we are both compassionate toward the homeless. I really miss her.

We head home to rest before dinner. Later this evening, the family is meeting up at a local restaurant to eat. Dad is paying for us all.

At the restaurant, Pastor David and Lady Patrice arrive with their tribe.

Did she go to the doctor to find out if she is really pregnant again? I wonder to myself. I forgot to ask her when I saw her at the daycare. I think I was trying to avoid any serious conversations.

"How are you, Ieshia?" David asks.

"I am blessed and highly favored," I say without blinking an eye. "How are you?"

"I am well," he says.

I look the other way and roll my eyes.

"This has got to stop. Why can't y'all get along?" Patrice asks.

I have had it with the reprimands. Maybe I am finally ready for the truth to come out.

"Ask your husband, Lady Patrice. Pastor David knows why I can't stand him."

"Ieshia! There are children at this table." Mom says. "What's the matter with you?"

"Ask your son-in-law and Associate Pastor what's wrong with me." I say with an attitude.

"Lord, take the wheel," Mom says.

Dinner ends early and we all go back to Mom and Dad's house. David and Patrice follow us inside.

Now I say what Mom always says, "Lord, take the wheel."

The kids go out back to play and all us adults go into Dad's office to talk. I am not ready for this, but it's time to tell my truth.

We sit at Dad's conference table, and he leads the discussion.

"Ieshia Sarah Harvey and Pastor David Sanders. We are family, and we have to right this wrong. Why can't y'all get along?"

"Pastor Sanders, should I tell 'im or you?"

Patrice looks confused, "What is going on? Let's back up to the other night. Who is your baby daddy? Dad, she said Demarcus is not Malcolm's father!"

"What?" Dad begins to yell. "Ieshia, what is going on? I know you all are adults, and have your right to privacy, but there will be no confusion in my house. Let's talk. We are the First Family and we will handle this tonight. David and I are about to go on a three-day revival to Jacksonville, Florida, and I need my house whole and healed before we leave. Ieshia, you always hold stuff in."

I drop my head and start crying, crying, crying, crying. It's as if my heart fell back into the same anxiety I had as a 16-year-old. But my mind gets a hold of me. I am a woman. I stand up. After ten long years I finally tell my story.

"I was raped one month before I was shipped to Atlanta."

"Raped?" Dad asked with a tone that says he doesn't believe me.

"Michael, shut up and let her talk," Mom finally stands up to him. "You shipped my baby off ten years ago without giving her a change to tell us what happened, and now she is back. Let her talk! It's about time!"

I start my story again. "I was raped at age sixteen, one month before I was shipped off to Atlanta. I had no idea I was pregnant. It all happened so quickly; I did not think I could be pregnant. I didn't know who to tell. I was violated and scared. I just put the incident in the back of my brain and went on. When my cycle stopped coming on that first month, I still didn't think I was pregnant. It all happened so fast."

I looked at David and said, "You took my virginity. You pervert."

David stands up and says, "You are lying!"

"David Sanders, you know what you did to me!"

He starts to shake his head and cut me off, but Mom silences him and I continue.

"I was home and you swung by and said you was here to pick up Patrice. Patrice was upstairs in the bathroom taking a shower. Mom and Dad were at a neighbor's house. I let you in the front door and left you in the living room.

"I went to my room to listen to my music as I always do. Patrice always took long showers and was singing her heart away. She was oblivious to what was going on right under her nose. I had my music on loud since Mom and Dad were gone, instead of me using my earbuds. I was dancing and twirling in my bedroom.

"When I turned around, you were in my room. I asked you, 'What do you want?' That's when you grabbed me and threw me on the bed. You ripped my shirt and held your hand over my mouth. You raped me!

"Come clean, Pastor David Sanders! From that day on I hated your guts. I never liked being around you."

"David," Patrice said, "you told me you were a virgin when we married."

"Virgin?" I interrupt. "Sis, David lost his virginity during basic training in the Army. You were the virgin on your honeymoon night, not him.

Dad stands up. "David!"

"Yes, sir?" David asks shyly.

"Is this true?"

David grabs his head. Very slowly he says, "Yes, sir. It is. I am so sorry. I can explain everything. I had been drinking and I lost it."

"I don't believe you, Ieshia!" Patrice jumps in. "How could you? This is my husband. Take a blood test! I demand it!"

Patrice and David stand up and leave abruptly.

● ● ●

Dad still went to do his three-day revival, but David stayed home. Patrice has had him on the sofa all week. I know because the kids told Malcolm their Dad had been sleeping on the sofa, but they didn't know why.

A week later the blood work is done, and its official. David is Malcolm's biological father.

Patrice goes to the doctor and is officially six weeks pregnant.

"Lawd, why?" I shake my head when I hear the news.

We gather again another week to try to work through the truth and find some kind of peace. We are back in

Dad's office, but this time the kids are all at Patrice's house with a babysitter.

Dad takes a deep breath and says, "We need to pray."

"We need to talk and pray," I said. "I was raped ten years ago by my sister's fiancé who is now her husband. He is a rapist that loves God and has a family." I try to give some grace along with the big shovelful of truth.

"David, what were you thinking?" Patrice asks with tears streaming down her face.

"I don't know. I messed up really bad. I was young and stupid. I have been repenting again, just like I did after it happened ten years ago."

"Who else have you bothered?" Patrice asks.

"Listen, I am not a molester, okay? She was the only one. I had a couple of drinks. I was intoxicated and feeling some stress from the upcoming wedding, building a new home for us, and all the pressure of measuring up to your dad as a young minister."

"I do remember you would drink every once in a while," Patrice says. "I never told anyone, but you stopped once we got married. I've never seen you drink since then," she said softly.

"When did you start drinking?" Dad asks.

"While I was in basic training and once I graduated and went to my first assignment. I hated being away from home and was missing Patrice. That is one reason I went from Active Duty to the Reserves. I feel horrible about everything that happened and have lived with this pain for years." He turns to me and continues to talk.

"When Patrice told me you were pregnant and that you had been shipped off, I knew it was my child."

Patrice and Mom begin to cry.

Dad starts to pray.

Patrice starts to sing quietly.

Mostly, we sit in the heavy stillness.

Dad then says, "David you are going to have to take a leave of absence from your duty as Associate Pastor, and you as well, Patrice, from your duty as Daycare Director. This is so you can work on your marriage and get some counseling. This is serious. This is the past that has leapt into our present.

"I don't hold judgment against anyone here. My heart is heavy, and I have forgiveness for all, except for myself. I now have to work to forgive myself for shipping my baby girl off for something she had no control over."

The Bridge

Chapter 7

At the age of 16, I had a lot to take in and consider. I was pregnant. I was a teenager. I was scared. I was ashamed. I was embarrassed. I had to start over. I was not ready to be a mom.

So many questions ran through my mind. I wrote them, along with my thoughts and prayers in my journal.

Why me? What did I do to deserve this? Who can I talk to? Will I survive? Will I endure? Will I be a good mom? What will my baby be like? How will I raise my child alone? I would like to do this with a mate. No one let me explain.

God, do You hear me? I mean, do You really hear me? I don't talk to You much, but I believe in You in my heart. It's me and You, I guess? I won't rush through my prayers anymore.

When will I see my parents again? Will I miss Patrice and David's wedding? How much weight will I pick up? I am dancer? Do I need to finish high school? Should I go to college?

I continued to write.

You know, this journaling is really helping. All of this was bottled up inside of my head. My emotions are everywhere. My nights are becoming restless.

My appetite is changing. I want more food. Burgers. Fries. Fast Food. That's the food I want for me, but it's not just me anymore, at least not for the next eight months. I got to eat healthy. I must eat healthy.

Aunt Velma, she is a God sent angel on earth. I need her just as much as she needs me.

Who else is a pregnant teen like me? Can we talk? Can we Facetime? Can we meet face-to-face?

Are these emotions and thoughts normal? I think they are. I don't even have a driver's license. I do have a learner's permit. I am almost legal.

I have to leave an inheritance for my child. That's in the Bible. See, God. I read your word sometimes. Okay, I hear you. I will try to do better.

I didn't ask for this. The baby didn't ask for this either. What we gonna do?

I stood up and stood as tall as I could. I went and stood in front of the mirror that was connected to the back of the dresser.

I saw a pregnant girl. I saw fear. I saw anxiety. I saw the unknown.

What a minute.

I remembered reading Maya Angelou poems in Mrs. Dixon's English class.

Still I rise. Still I rise. Still I rise. Still I rise.

I am feeling better. Something is rising up in me. Is that the Holy Ghost power Daddy preached about?

I chuckled as tears poured and fell from my face. I stood tall and stretched as if I were in dance class. I turned on some music and I danced away. I danced, and danced, and danced.

Dad always said to dance like King David danced, but his dance was different. King David had his day in the Bible, but this was my moment. King David made some mistakes, but God always provided a way of escape for him. I could relate to King David. Our struggles were different, but as I danced, I felt liberated.

As I danced, I formulated new ideas in my mind. As I danced, I differentiated truth from lies. As I danced, I administrated justice. As I danced, I appropriated responsibility. As I danced, I began the process of forgiveness.

I kept dancing, dancing, dancing, dancing, dancing . . . Then I took a leap in the air. I did a huge kick. I landed on the ground perfectly and took a deep breath.

I heard applause behind me. I turned around. It was Aunt Velma, Pedro, and Ms. Joiner. I did not know I had an audience!

Aunt Velma came up to hug me. I was hot and sweaty.

"Ieshia Sarah Harvey," she said, "this was my first time seeing you dance, and I am smitten by your talent. Girl! You got talent. Keep dancing please! Never let it die." She cried and hugged me again. "Girl, you got game!"

I smiled and said, "Thank you."

The next morning, we woke up and ate breakfast. Ms. Joiner came back to cook breakfast for us. I had to get dressed to go see my OB/GYN. Her name was Dr. Jay. I really liked her.

She gave me a lot of stuff to read and signed me up for group talk sessions at a facility for teenage moms. They met once a month.

Then it was off to school. I made sure to grab my doctor's excuse for missing school my first morning. Aunt Velma dropped me off at Hinesville Academy, and said she would be back to pick me up at the end of the day.

I missed riding the bus, but it was different here. I learned to adjust and to be more grateful for support.

I took a deep breath and walked into the building. I entered into the main office. The student intern, Kelly, from the other day was there.

"Hi."

"Good morning."

I turned in my doctor's note and Kelly gave me a hall pass. Oh, they forgot to make a Student ID card for me, so I stayed in the main office a little longer than anticipated.

"Thanks, Kelly," I said as she handed me my freshly printed ID.

I went to my assigned classes, but before lunch I got permission to go see the school nurse, Nurse Richards. I really liked her.

I updated her on my doctor's appointment and shared the literature I got. She was glad I was moving forward and came to see her. I told her I was really excited about the teen parent group meetings.

I headed back to class before the bell dismissed us for lunch.

"Hi, can you show me how to get to the cafeteria?" I asked a nearby girl. "This school is so large; I can't remember my way even though I saw it on the tour yesterday."

"Yes, follow me."

"I am Ieshia."

"I am Amy."

"What's up."

"You the new kid?"

"Word gets around."

"Yeah."

"We heard you can dance?"

I chuckled. "Yeah, a little something like that."

"You can sit with us at lunch."

"Word."

Lunch was a lot better than I anticipated. Maybe it was because my attitude had changed, and I was feeling hopeful. I had never been afraid of people before anyway. I usually talked a lot, like my Dad, but at this school, I was laying low.

I have to smoke 'em out, I thought. *You know, that spiritual discernment thing.*

Next, I moved on to dance class. I was so excited and ready. I walked into the studio and the dance instructor, Ms. Nichols, pulled me aside.

"Hi, Ieshia. We provide dance attire for you. We receive funding from a philanthropist foundation that left 3.7 million dollars to fund our theater and dance program. My assistant, Mr. Johnson, will assign you a locker and rehearsal gear."

"Thank you, Instructor Nichols," I say.

The assistant gave me some gear. It was enough attire to last a week. I immediately slip into the restroom to switch into my leotard and tights.

Wow. I think I am going to like Hinesville Academy.

I walked into the studio and stood with the rest of the class. Ms. Nichols approached the front of the room and said, "Class, let's welcome Ieshia."

They all clapped.

"She is a new student at our school and will be a part of our dance studio." She looked at me and said, "Show me what you got!"

I didn't back down. Mr. Johnson, her assistant, turned on some music. Ms. Nichols started dancing to the theme music of Swan Lake Ballet, and I joined her. She was impressed. The music then changed to an African Style mixed with some Caribbean beats. Ms. Nichols kept dancing.

White girl got some skills.

Two students joined in. Kelly, the office intern, was one of them.

I clapped back with my skills.

I am crunk now.

Ms. Nichols shouted, "Are you ready for another round?"

"So, you think you can dance?" I responded.

"Last round," Mr. Johnson said, and he turned the music up even louder. It was hip-hop music, and my favorite artist, Drake. It was really on now. I showed my skills.

Dre's home lessons came in handy. The entire class joined in and start dancing.

Okay, I am all in!

At the end, we all clapped. Everyone came up and told me their names. I was now an official dance student at Hinesville Academy. We got back into formation and the instructor started with the teaching part of our class.

She not only taught us movement; she taught us theory as well. It made me appreciate the art of dance even more. Class came to an end, and we changed out of our dance gear. The studio classroom had a locker room complete with showers and all.

They ain't playing.

I showered, dressed, and went out front to wait on Aunt Velma to pick me up. I was tired and thirsty. I grabbed a bottle of water from my bag.

• • •

The days, weeks, months, and seasons began to roll like they were hours, minutes, and seconds.

Atlanta had everything. The Atlanta Braves. The Atlanta Hawks. The CNN Center. It was all there, and time waited for on no one. We stayed busy.

Aunt Velma loved music concerts, so we went to several. We always had front row tickets. Most of the time, we went to the Opera and Jazz, but sometimes she would switch it up. We have seen Jay-Z, Ciara, John Legend, and Justin Timberlake.

Outside of entertainment with Aunt Velma London, my life was fairly routine: school, doctor appointments, dance class, daily visits to the school nurse, and, oh, how can I forget church? Aunt Velma was big on that.

I was also growing. I mean, I was really growing. I did not look the same. I had been taking pictures of myself each month. Wow. Being pregnant really changes the body.

My dance routine and mechanisms developed, but now at six months pregnant, I had to modify my moves.

Mom had been calling and I sent her some pics of myself. I loved hearing her voice. She cried every time we talked. Me being away was really hard for her.

Patrice and David were officially husband and wife. My Patrice was now officially Lady Sanders. I was happy for her. Mom managed to make me a copy of the wedding DVD and mailed it to me. She even sent some of the photos.

Getting out of bed in the mornings was becoming more and more difficult. I was sleepy and tired. I found out I was carrying a boy. I eventually wore full-blast maternity clothes.

My son was very active in my belly. He kicked me often, and I felt him moving when I would go to dance.

I made sure to read him a bedtime story each night. I started praying more every day and went to church with Aunt Velma each Sunday. We attended a virtual Bible Study on Wednesday evenings, which was fine with me.

Her church, Faith Cathedral, was huge and they streamed their services live every Sunday and Wednesday on their website. They had over 3,000 members. I didn't know anybody there, but I made the best of it. Everybody knew Aunt Velma at the church. It was not traditional at all, and far from being Baptist. That was fine with me.

I was experiencing new things and growing in every area of my life. In three months, I would be a mom. Wow. I was almost to the finish line!

Aunt Velma and I finally went shopping to set up the nursery. Malcolm, my baby, would be in my room after he arrived. When he turned about six weeks old, he would move across the hall to the nursery.

Aunt Velma told me that Dad had been wiring money to her each month. I was glad to hear that. I knew he would do his part, but why wouldn't he call me? I still loved him. Did he love me? Oh, well.

Everyone at school was so supportive. My dance routine had changed drastically, but I was still going to class. I could no longer do a lot of the dances, but I still got my exercise in. Around the seventh month, my dance class threw a baby shower for me. Dean Thomas approved it, and it was so nice I cried. Aunt Velma, Pedro, and Ms. Joiner came too.

One Sunday, Aunt Velma was not feeling well, so we stayed in. Ms. Joiner came over to cook breakfast and lunch. She made me a turkey and cheese omelet with mushrooms and spinach. I drank a glass of apple juice and took my prenatal vitamins.

We watched virtual church online. Lunch was a turkey sandwich and a bowl of fruit. For dinner, Ms. Joiner made some vegetable soup with crackers and peanut butter and jelly sandwiches. I had not had that simple meal since I left home months before.

Aunt Velma and I had a conversation about daycare. The OB/GYN gave me some options to look at, as did the school nurse. They were all high-end expensive. Growing up back home, Mother Gladys kept us when Mama had to run errands while she was a stay-at-home mom. When each of us turned three-years-old, Mom enrolled us into daycare, so I was open to the idea, but I didn't know how I could afford it.

Aunt Velma had a plan, as always. She said Uncle Ricky was a planner and he taught her strategic planning. She wanted to pay for an in-house nanny after I had Malcolm. The nanny would watch him while I was at school. When he turned one-year-old, the plan was to send him to a daycare.

Wow! I didn't know that was an option! "Let's do it," I said.

She set up some interviews and we worked as a team one Saturday morning to interview five ladies. Pedro and Ms. Joiner sat in on the interview committee as well. She valued their input.

I thought Pedro liked the housemaid, Ms. Joiner. I saw them talking one day on the patio. Ms. Joiner had made Pedro a glass of lemonade. They sat and chatted for a long time. I don't miss much.

We narrowed the nanny list down to two ladies. Aunt Velma agreed to hire both part-time, and they would split the days each week. Aunt Velma still stayed in contact with the Law Firm Uncle Ricky worked at before he died. One of the lawyers reviewed the hiring paperwork and provided some additional consultation.

Aunt Velma always went all the way. She had payroll set up and everything. The nannies signed contracts and planned to return once I came home with the baby. Oh, Aunt Velma also had background checks completed. She don't play. Plus, the nannies didn't know about the cameras.

• • •

"Aunt Velma!" I yelled. "AUNT VELMA!"

Crap she upstairs in her penthouse bedroom. She can't hear me.

I called her cell phone. She answered and I said, "It's time."

She ran to my bedroom, sprinting down those stairs like she was on a track team.

"My water just broke."

I was calm but scared too. I had finally made it to forty weeks on the dot when my water broke. My hospital bag was already packed. Aunt Velma grabbed the bag, and we headed to the car.

On the way to the hospital, she called Mom and told her the baby was coming. We arrived at the hospital early Friday morning around 4:30 a.m. It was early, early, early.

We walked into the emergency room and checked in.

Those contractions! There was nothing like it. I remembered my breathing exercises from Lamaze classes. I had also picked up a lot of pointers when I attended my monthly teen parent meetings. They were a life saver.

My OB/GYN, Dr. Jay, came in to check me.

"Ieshia, how are you feeling?"

"Ready to have this baby."

Malcolm would be there soon. Six hours later, he arrived.

Malcolm Jamal Harvey, 7 pounds, 4 ounces.

Something in me told me Malcolm was my first and last child. I think I received that message after those contractions!

How did I pick his name? I loved watching reruns of The Bill Cosby show with Mom. Theo, Bill and Clare Huxtable's son, was my favorite character. I named Malcolm after the actor who played Theo on the show.

Forgiveness

Chapter 8

In Dad's office, after Dad finishes praying and Patrice finishes singing. We are all in tears. We all hug, and Patrice and David go home.

At this point, I don't know what to say or do. I had the same feeling I had that day in the hospital when I discovered that I was pregnant.

I do feel better now that everything is out in the open, but the journey of moving forward is going to be a hard one.

"Ieshia," Dad says. "We need to talk."

Finally. It only took ten years.

We go sit on the front porch. Mom went up to bed early. After all of the tension, she caught a headache and said she was tired.

"Ieshia Sarah Harvey, I am so sorry. I feel like I am responsible for all of this. I never gave you time or even an opportunity to respond or tell your side of what happened. When your Mom called me and said you were pregnant, I was furious and embarrassed. I was too angry to talk, so I took action.

"I called your Aunt Velma and she said you could come and live with her for a while. I never knew you would be gone for ten long years.

"What was I thinking? I just assumed it was Demarcus' baby. Now everything is coming together. When I called his mom and told her, she was perplexed.

"She told me, *'Pastor Harvey, my son has not slept with your daughter. When he told me he was dating her, I jacked him up early and told him no sex, and if he ever wanted to have sex to leave her alone and go find somebody else to sleep with.'*

"I thought maybe she missed it or something. That maybe she thought too well of her son. I even spoke with him a couple of times after you left and he kept saying, 'Sir, I know what this looks like, but we never had sex.'

"I just pushed what they said away as lies, trying to get out of responsibility. You went away and I went on with ministry and life. Okay. Let's hear from you."

Now it is my turn. I have had this conversation so many times in my head, but I am now speechless.

Jesus, be a fence.

That's something Mother Gladys would say when she would babysit Patrice and I after I would smart off.

I take three deep breaths. I do that a lot to gather myself and focus.

"Dad, it's been ten years. I have a lot to say." Tears begin to form in my eyes. "I was hurt, confused, and lost. I had been raped and had not told anybody. When I tried to speak, no one would listen. Then I was shipped off, put on a Greyhound bus with my luggage to face a new city and new life without my parents.

"Aunt Velma was a jewel. She was my blessing in the middle of a blessing. She planted seed into Malcolm and I. Atlanta became our rescue and safe haven. I never looked back. After having Malcolm, I stayed in high school. I was tested for the gifted program and began taking Advanced and Advanced Placement courses before graduating. I finished high school and Malcolm took off growing as a little boy. I surrounded myself with him and dance.

"Aunt Velma really wanted me to go to the local community college, but college was not for me. Aunt Velma was my rock and still is. When Malcolm was five, and I had been out of high school for about four years, I decided to move out. It was a big step, but I needed to develop my own space. Aunt Velma helped me purchase a small dance studio that included a two-bedroom apartment in downtown Atlanta. I obtained a small business loan with her as my co-signer. She wanted to pay for it, but I refused. She had been so gracious. I wanted ownership and responsibility.

"Hinesville Academy, my high school alma mater, funded a grant program that channeled youth to my dance studio. That program lasted until Malcolm was about nine and a half years old, and then it ended.

"I became behind on my mortgage and it looked like I was going to have move back in with Aunt Velma. Thankfully, an industry bought out the block, and I got a nice return on my investment property.

"I did move back in with Aunt Velma, but after living with her for about six months, I was led to come home. We called Mom, packed up, and now we are here.

"I had to face my past in order to move forward. I am older, wiser, and more mature. Your baby girl grew up. I am a woman now. I am glad we talked, Dad. The pain was gone for a while, but it did resurface."

Dad begins to cry. I give him a hug. This is it! In that moment, Dad begins to talk again with tears rolling down his face.

"I am so sorry, Ieshia. I am so sorry, Ieshia. I am so, so sorry, Ieshia. Please forgive me."

"I do," I say. "Let's move forward. Remember those sermons you have preached over the years? Let's live 'em through forgiveness."

We both head up to bed. I shower, put on my gown, and get in bed. Then I get back up and start dancing. As I dance, I remember dancing in my room as a child and teenager. I remember the laughs I had with Patrice and running up the stairs to avoid house chores. I finally get back into the bed and fall asleep.

The next morning, Dad runs into my room and says, "Your mother is not breathing."

"What?" I get up and immediately run to their room.

Malcolm hears the commotion and gets up too. We call the ambulance and they come, but it's too late.

The paramedics did all they could to revive her. Mom, Michelle Ann Harvey, died of a heart attack.

God! What are you doing? I can't take this. What are you doing? You told me to come back home, and I did. Now this?

I call Patrice and tell her.

She screams. They all come over.

Dad is numb. He calls the local funeral home to make arrangements. Of course, because Mom was a First Lady, the funeral is going to be huge.

The church staff asks the church members and local neighbors to wait a day or two before they come over, but when do black folks ever listen? They start coming over after lunch.

Aunt Velma gets the news and drives down. I am so glad to see her. Having to make arrangements is hard when death is sudden. I did not even get to say good-bye. At least Malcolm got to know Mom and spend some time with her.

Patrice isn't saying much to me and I am good with that. She has a lot to deal with. Her husband is the father of her sister's son. She is pregnant, and now Mom has died. No one saw this coming.

Calls, calls, calls, and more calls. People brought food over to the house for days. The community is generous with food donations.

Mom was well known in the community. Three days after her death, we have the funeral. It was a day no one was prepared for.

The funeral limousines arrive. There are two. Dad's armorbearers are still scurrying about. They are now Associate Ministers. By the time we hit the church parking lot, they are opening the limo doors for Dad and us.

We proceed into the church as a family, while the choir sings, *We Shall Wear a Crown.*

Mom is laying so lovely in her blue casket.

The kids all take it really hard.

David is numb. Patrice will not let him console her at all.

We get through the funeral, and now we go to the grave site.

Aunt Velma is with Dad the entire time. After the funeral, we go back to the church fellowship hall to eat. It's been remodeled sometime in the past ten years. It is now a large room and has flat screen monitors on the wall.

I find humor in everything I can.

The food is really good.

Dr. Stanley is there and comes over to say hello.

There that nerd go again.

Several of the homeless people from the shelter are present. They look so distinguished and dressed up. Are those Uncle Ricky's suits I see on them? I remember the conversation Aunt Velma and I had when I first went to live with her in Atlanta.

They are probably not his suits, but some kind soul donated them.

We eventually go back home. It's not the same without her, my Mom. Her presence is still so very strong in the house. I feel the brokenness. I am in my bedroom, alone.

Malcolm had been asking if he could spend the night with his Aunt Patrice to play with his cousins and I thought this would be a good night for him to go, at least for me—probably not for Patrice.

Aunt Velma comes in. She sits on the bed beside me and gives me a big hug.

"I am going to be here a while to help out," she says. "What's going on with you? It's more than your Mom, I can tell."

I tell her everything. She is shocked and pissed. She says some choice words. I hope Dad doesn't hear her. I love her humor. She was sipping on something too, and it was not lemonade.

How is it going to work with her in Dad's house? This is going to be interesting.

Redemption

Chapter 9

One week after Mom's funeral, I decide to enroll Malcolm into a summer camp until we can figure out this thing called life. He needs some socialization and instruction while out of school for the summer. I don't play about those grades and learning. He has made straight A's since kindergarten.

Dad has been in his room most of the day. I know he's grieving.

The Executive Pastor, Samuel Bivins, is overseeing the church while Dad is out, and while Pastor David is on his leave of absence. Pastor Bivins is an older gentleman around Dad's age.

David and Patrice come over.

"Please don't say anything," I say to Aunt Velma.

"Girl," Aunt Velma replies, "You know I am the sassy one, but I will try."

"Patrice is heartbroken and has been crying for weeks. I don't want to add to my sister's pain."

David goes up to see Dad.

Is that a good thing or bad thing? Well, oh well.

Patrice and I sit in the living room to chat. Patrice is still crying. She is taking everything really hard. She cries a long time. We are almost out of Kleenex. Finally, she starts talking.

"Let's move forward, Ieshia. This is so hard for me. I am now two months pregnant. My Mom has died. My husband raped my sister when she was a teenager. I feel so stuck and violated.

"All of the missing pieces and questions I had about your radical behavior toward David now make sense. I never would have thought in a million years that I was married to a rapist. I don't know what to do.

"I love that man. We have been together for ten years. He has been good to me and the family. He is a hard worker and always comes through for us. I never saw this coming.

"He had a hidden issue that came to surface. We are in counseling, but it's not helping me at all. He is still sleeping on the sofa. Lord, come through for me. Lord, I need you to come through for me right now."

She drops her head in agony. There is silence in the room.

I am dried up and out of tears. I cried for years and now they are crying.

Lord, how do we fix this wrong?

"Patrice," I say as I grab her hands and look at her in her eyes. "Jesus Christ hung on the cross for our sins that we might live again. The blood He shed at Calvary was for us all. By His stripes we are healed. By His stripes we are set free. By His stripes, He gives us a new life in Him.

"David made one dreadful mistake ten years ago. He had been drinking, but there is no excuse for what he did! Still, we must find forgiveness in our hearts. I have. It took me years, but I have forgiven. I still had to tell the truth. Forgiving doesn't take away the truth or the consequences.

"That one wrong he did does not take away from all the good he has done. Yes, this is a big pill to swallow, but there is something God wants us to learn in all of this. God has forgiven David, and we must do the same."

I give her a big hug. I sound like Mom.

Where did all that come from?

David and Dad come downstairs. Aunt Velma comes in from the kitchen and says it's time to eat. She fixed a tossed salad and baked a cake.

Dad asks David to say the prayer.

He says, "Let us pray." He takes a deep breath and starts crying. "Lord, please forgive me. I made a huge mistake many years ago. It has haunted me for years. I want my life restored and my family back. I love Patrice and my children. I am not a rapist. I did a major wrong. Please, please forgive me."

Patrice starts crying again. The Kleenex are gone. Let me grab some napkins.

David can't finish his prayer. He gets up and lifts his hands to the sky in surrender to God. Dad gets up and goes over to hug him.

Aunt Velma start speaking in tongues.

Now, that's a first. It must be the Hennessey she mixed in with her sweet tea. I saw her; I don't miss much. It's all coming together.

Aunt Velma says grace over the food, and we eat. It feels like old times but it's not the same without Mom. We must be hungry because the salad is gone.

Aunt Velma gets up again. "I have an announcement to make." We all smile. "After much prayer, I have decided to move back to Dublin. After Ieshia and Malcolm moved back here it was not the same at my house. Coming home for the funeral and seeing family and friends, made me realize what I need most.

"I've been on the phone a lot since the funeral. Those phone calls have been in reference to my property and real estate. I am a very wealthy lady. God has been good to me and to Ricky, when he was alive.

"I am selling the house to Ms. Joiner. She has been my housemaid for years. She finally told me that she and Pedro are dating and considering marriage. I will go back later to pack up my things. I will auction off some of the furniture, but Ms. Joiner will keep most of it.

"Ricky's suits have been donated to a local charity to assist young men to find jobs and I even packed up some and brought then down to the homeless shelter Michelle was running. We had many conversations, and she was so glad Ieshia and Malcolm had come back home to stay. I have talked with your Dad and will be staying with him for a while. I will eventually find me a home to stay in."

I go over and give Aunt Velma a big kiss. We finish dinner, Dad and David go to his study, and us ladies start to clean the kitchen.

"Ieshia, your Dad has asked me to help out at the shelter for a while. Will you come and work with me?" Aunt Velma asks.

"Sure, I will, but only temporarily."

"Girl, come on now."

"I know. I want to open a Dance Studio."

"What's stopping you?"

"I never thought about that."

Aunt Velma is a on roll. "Patrice, your dad told me you and David are on a leave of absence. Take as much time as you need to work on your marriage."

"Thanks, Aunt Velma."

"Make it work. He really loves you and wants to remain your husband. Whatever you decide to do moving forward, we will support you.

"Alright girls, how am I supposed to tell your Dad I got some Hennessey and wine up in here?"

"I already know, Big Sis." We turn around and see Dad standing at the kitchen entrance door. We all laugh.

"Velma, I am so glad you decided to move back home. I love you, even with that Hennessey and wine, all the same."

Weeks pass and Aunt Velma and I tag team to work at the homeless shelter. Mom had a dynamic set up and her staff is sensational. They are trained and handle the clientele so well.

Dr. Stanley from the school system comes through twice a week to teach GED classes. He is still nerdy.

It's time for the annual fundraiser for the Homeless Shelter. Aunt Velma and the office staff plan it. The shelter program is grant-funded but additional donations are always needed.

Aunt Velma asks me to dance for the fundraiser. I agree. The event is held at the shelter, but everyone is in shirt and tie. Dad is the guest speaker. He has not been preached since Mom died. It's been about one and a half months. It's time.

He has still been going to weekly worship, but Pastor Bivins has been bringing the word. Daddy needed a break. He rarely took time off when we were growing up. We would manage to get in one summer trip each year. That was it.

After Dad speaks, I come up to dance. I dance to Jill Scott, *A Long Walk*. It feels so good to be dancing. My mind goes back to when I was a little girl and dancing as

I was carrying Malcolm. At the end of my performance, the audience gives me a standing applause.

After the event, Dr. Stanley, comes up and says, "I didn't know you danced."

"I do."

"Would you like to go for coffee sometime?"

That is such a lame pick up line. I will give him an A for effort. He tried. He growing on me.

"What about a movie and a dinner?"

"Yes."

"That would be nice. I will have to check my calendar and get back with you," he says.

This joker here. He need me in his life.

"Dr. Stanley," I say with charm, "What about tomorrow?"

"I think that will work."

• • •

When it comes to family, all of us adults have worked through our differences, but the children still don't know the truth about David being Malcolm's biological father.

How do we do handle this? We decide to all go over to David and Patrice's house on a Saturday afternoon.

Patrice is cooking and pregnant. Now she is the one who is growing. We all eat and now it's time for dessert. We call the children in from the backyard. We begin to tell them that Malcolm is their brother.

"I already know," Malcolm says.

"Malcolm, be quiet and let me talk," I say.

"Mama, my cousins—sisters and brothers—told me last month. That's why Uncle David has been sleeping on the sofa. We know, and I am cool with Uncle Dad."

I take a deep breath and look at my son.

"Can we go back outside and play?"

They leave to go play.

We were not expecting that at all. The perfect set up by God. Won't He do it!

Welcome to My Future

Chapter 10

A lot has happened since I moved back to Dublin, Georgia one year ago. Malcolm is now in 6th grade. He is training to be Dad's new armor bearer. He tried out for basketball and made the team.

Patrice gave birth to her fifth child and she is pregnant again!

I have opened my dance studio, Dancin' in the Rain. It is going quite well. I now have a waiting list. I offer more day classes and have teachers on staff to help with the classes. I no longer offer weekend classes. My dance instructor from high school, Ms. Reeves, came down and is assisting me at the dance studio. She still got made skills.

Aunt Velma is my part-time office manager once again. She stepped down from being Interim Director of the homeless shelter and recommended Mom's Assistant Director take the lead. Aunt Velma didn't want anything to tie her up from her new beau. Yes, she is dating the Executive Pastor, Samuel Bivins. He is six years younger than her and she is loving every minute of it. She is still hanging on to her Hennessey and wine.

Dad and the entire family went on a cruise to the Bahamas. Once we got back, he became acquainted with Ms. Berry. She works at the local school board office and is a widow as well. We are happy for him. They are spending time together, but he says it is nothing serious. They go out every week.

I finally called Dre' and we had a very long conversation. He now knows everything. He is happily married, and I enjoyed meeting his wife and family. He goes to church and is training to be a Deacon. He mentors young guys at the local Department of Juvenile Justice. His dad is finally out of prison and lives with him.

As for my love life, I am getting ready to walk down the aisle to marry Dr. Stanley, the man I bumped into at the school board office a year ago. We finally went on our date, and another date, and another date. He is loosening up. I became his fire and he became my everything.

I will be starting college classes after we get back from our honeymoon. I plan to major in Theater. It's never too late for anything.

I am Ieshia Sarah Harvey and I approve this message.

About the Author

Yasmin Whirl is a native of Toomsboro, Georgia, and the daughter of Willie C. and Irene Strange. She has two sisters, a niece, and two nephews.

She currently resides in Dublin, Georgia, and has worked in education for 22 years in the Wilkinson County School District.

She is a author, motivator, and minister. Her passion for Christ has afforded her the opportunity to work in Children's Ministry, Music Ministry, Intercessory Prayer, Church Leadership/Administration, and Singles Ministry.

She holds a Doctorate and Specialist Degree in Educational Leadership, a Specialist and Master's Degree in Counseling, and a Bachelor's Degree in Sociology. In 2019, she graduated from Interdenominational Theological Center with a certificate in Theology. She is a proud member of Alpha Kappa Alpha Sorority, Inc.

In 2018, she was honored to travel abroad and preach the gospel in Johannesburg, South Africa. Philippians 4:13 is her motto: "I can do all things through Christ who strengthens me."

Follow Yasmin Whirl on social media:

Twitter @ywhirl
Instagram @ywhirl
Facebook Yasmin Whirl

www.OurWrittenLives.com